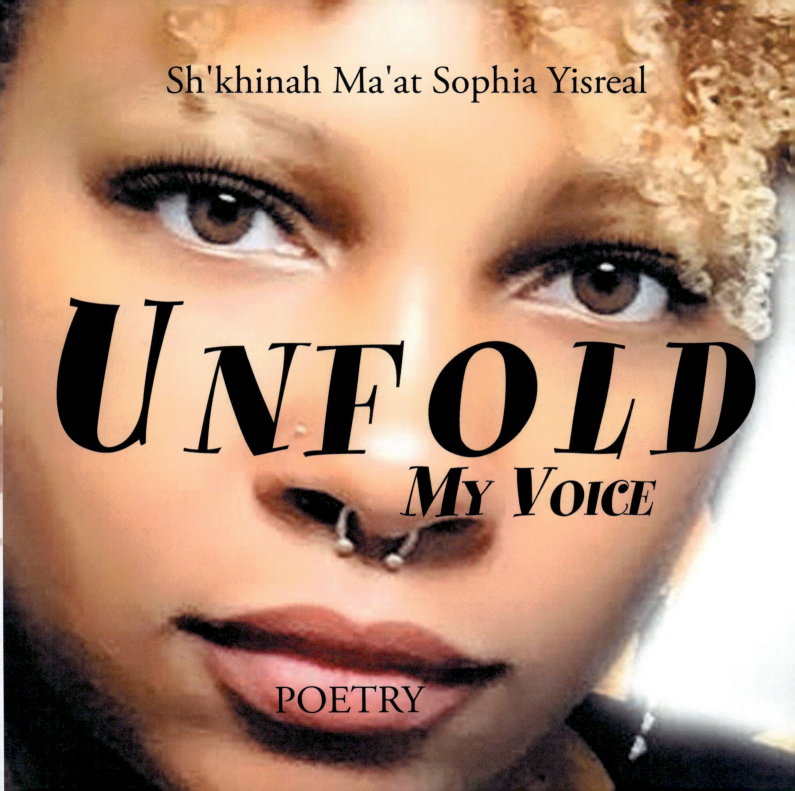

Sh'khinah Ma'at Sophia Yisreal

UNFOLD
MY VOICE

POETRY

Order this book online at www.trafford.com
or email orders@trafford.com

Most Trafford titles are also available at major online book retailers.

 www.trafford.com

North America & international
toll-free: 1 888 232 4444 (USA & Canada)
fax: 812 355 4082

Our mission is to efficiently provide the world's finest, most comprehensive book publishing service, enabling every author to experience success. To find out how to publish your book, your way, and have it available worldwide, visit us online at www.trafford.com

Because of the dynamic nature of the Internet, any web addresses or links contained in this book may have changed since publication and may no longer be valid. The views expressed in this work are solely those of the author and do not necessarily reflect the views of the publisher, and the publisher hereby disclaims any responsibility for them.

Any people depicted in stock imagery provided by Getty Images are models,
and such images are being used for illustrative purposes only.
Certain stock imagery © Getty Images.

ISBN: 978-1-6987-0111-0 (sc)
ISBN: 978-1-6987-0110-3 (e)

Print information available on the last page.

Trafford rev. 05/19/2020

UNFOLD

MY VOICE

MA'AT THE POET
SH'KHINAH MA'AT SOPHIA YISREAL

UNFOLD

MY VOICE

To the monsters that started dismantling me; for my husband who helps reveal the light within me.

EDITOR NOTES

As the readers observe the style of poetry the author is using, her preference is Freestyle poetry. The writer did not want to be locked into a time loop of complaisance that can occur during writing. Freestyle writing is without a script pattern, rhythm sequence, and has no limitations. One note to know is the spelling of color, is spelled colour, which is Canadian.

DEDICATION

To my Mom,

You scared away the buggy man
that invaded my soul.
I will never forget your strength.

To my dad,
You supported your daughters even when
You didn't want to. It took a while; however,
I understand your view.

Love you both

_ ACKNOWLEDGMENTS _

I want to start off by giving my wonderful husband, Adam, a thank you for helping me with my book. It meant a lot to me for the support through all the long mornings and nights reading, editing, and being hard on myself. It was an emotional twister, I love you.

I do want to thank our boys Jerry, Kempous, Kevin, and Keshyon for showing so much love after all I have been through. You guys were young when the buggy men showed their faces. Thank you for being there as you got older to understand.

Again, I Want to bring acknowledgment to my mom for being there. You helped me out of some situations that I couldn't escape on my own. I love you mom.

To my sisters Marsh and Felicia, I know we didn't grow up close; however, I love you both.

Finally, Yahweh "The Most High", Thank you!

PREFACE

It felt as if the world turned its back on me, embracing me underneath the fire that wouldn't extinguish. The Smelling of my burnt flesh would follow me where ever I went. Seeing nothing to my anguish, I was always alone in my reflective time travel; seeing nothing but danger around every instance. With one son on my left, one son to my right, I had to mask my identity of black eyes, endless threats, and suicidal thoughts with taking my last breath...

I have been shelved, collecting dust, only to come in contact with elusive cheaters that made it look like Microfabric cloth. Derailed me in my healing, showing me that I'm one of the unwanted yet, lusted after. My cosmic energy has been affected by the unknown, the betrayal, and the feeling of being robbed within this vessel. Read the stories within my words. I felt as if I was in prison, and the guards would not release me.

Life was showing me its backhand, and it landed every time. I was accepting my life as a battered young woman. Nowhere to hide, yet in my mind of safety; a colourless foundation with the structure of unstable cracks...

Finding safety from the monsters that enslaved me, my mother that birthed me, pulled me out from underneath their regime. Years of battling the depression, threats, thoughts of suicide, being followed, and looking over my shoulders shaped me into the woman I have become. Trying to still illuminate on my own, seeing more of a colourful life, only to come into another emotional phase.

My life has been textured with cuts that have not fully HEALED, YET reshaped by new ideas. My husband told me during a visit, "You cannot forget and erase, but you can forgive and replace" (Adam Collins).

Contents

INTRODUCTION

Growing up, there were so many layers to understanding life. I was quiet and a hermit among myself. Being a tomboy and shy, no one knew what to expect from me which made me a target for insinuations.

The bullies played a part in my life's struggles, the boys increased my insecurities and inferior complex, the rap videos made me aware of my body, and family awakened me of my differences. I knew I was different, weird is what I've been called, but that didn't stop me from being myself. I accepted being called weird, it was part of my DNA. Being me was one thing I had that no one could take, so I thought.

Life exposed me to so many variables. the one variable that started my life was when sex was introduced to me. I was fourteen, thinking it's going to be a magical moment like on TV. His name was Tony and I met him through a class mate at her house. It was in a messy bedroom on a bunk bed. I didn't know this man and I introduced him to my body. His demeanor should have told me that this experience was not going to be one to tell my friends.

There was an excruciating pain going through my body as he tried to insert himself in me. He asked, "was I a virgin" and I nodded. I was scared to stop him; he proceeded to break through me as if I didn't matter. I bolted my eyes, desiring he would STOP. tunneling into his forearms with my nails and tears draining fiercely down my face.

My first encounter was not graceful, nor impressionable by any means. This was the catalyst that set the foot prints for future events to come.

ma'at the poet

•CHAPTER ONE•

UNFAMILIAR LOVE CAN UNDRESS
YOU AND LEAVE YOU NAKED.

CAUSE AND EFFECT

This realm Is DIGESTING me slowly,
tearing ME apart mentally,
I want to physically be appealing to the one that matters,
with no deliberations on side eyeing the different,
I tune my forks TO your vibrations,
I pay attention to YOUR movements and clarifications,
don't be distracted by the NEWNESS of others,
because you will lose the one that you're making invisible,
ME.

WHAT LIES WITHIN

You'll never *KNOW THE* intensity that
lies beneath my *INNER* being,
A shallow *HEART* rectifies a soundless woman's appealing,
Everything that surrounds me,
I walk with my head down low,
Catching a glimpse *OF* everyone's face,
that somehow just don't know,
Confusion sets in, wonder why things are to be,
Negative thoughts of suicide take over the *PURITY*,
A vision in the mirror stare back at me,
with a desperate look on her face,
Staring into hazel eyes waiting to know my place,
Sudden darkness overtakes me,
Not realizing what had befallen,
Perception of depression and degradation,
had become my calling,
Is God going to allow me to take my worth,
pity sets in, I flop to my knees,
Feeling I have to *LOVE* God first.

UNWANTED ENTRY

Searching the air for words that are incognito to my needs,
Liberating confusions,
SOMEHOW my mind has fought through THE weeds,
Captivating FIGURES invades blackened visions,
Rendering me helpless and powerless to my intentions,
Liquidizing my eyes when my soul wept,
INVADING MY spirit as I slept,
Excruciating fire penetrating within me,
Spreading apart the liquid sea,
That I didn't agree,
Too,
Let you in,
Your animalistic tendency's crept in,
Unaware of the storm clouds that are circling by,
I evade my THOUGHTS and go to an eccentric realm,
Feeling for the moment that the waves would end,
SLOWLY taking a piece of me at every second,
Popping the top to your indentation,
I LAY in motionless,
Never to heal,
Holding on to the edge of anything that seems to appeal,
To MY,
Silent screams to nurture my very ESSENCE,
Taken from this body my natural iridescence,
Uploading the normal that I once knew,
You took something from me,
One day someone will take something from you.

HER HEART

Blank mind flux of a woman under construction,
Confuting the CRACKS OF HER heart's irruption,
Balancing the BEAUTY of the invading beast,
Her heart IS not at peace,
A tort composition in a word,
no options,
Pursuing the BROKEN pieces of her domain intrusion,
Ignoring the face of the past,
The original monster,
She's trying to help the organically deep reflection,
Just to get one night of good sleep with no interception,
Tempted with the heart that's sorting the torn channels,
Fighting the drops that line the panels,
Should she roll the ball and let it glide,
Risk it all or run and hide,
She'll never know unless she tests the waters and sees,
She can't be scared of what it turns out to be,
Keep going and don't look back,
Don't look back.

WONDERING

Staying in my lane,
To show mercy on my lack of confidence,
I find the mind immersed in thought,
Fighting to come back,
To self,
The self that is unknown to me,
Rising from the dark,
An inner character shield,
The fragile to become impassive,
To the bull shit that is networked,
Over time,
That paradigm,
Shifts to an ugly confident woman,
That you call ugly black woman,
I hide behind,
The impressions of this character,
To illuminate my masked figure,
Shading the known symbolic jesters of,
The pillars embedded faith,
Intertwining the movements inside of me,
I stay in my lane,
To show mercy on my lack of confidence.

INSIDE OF ME

Chapters of my innocence Dwindle away deep within me,
The fire that burned Flamed out,
Aggressively,
Can you look me IN MY eyes and tell me what you see?
The woman in front of you,
Is it the person that seems to be free?
Can you identify the PAIN that is drawn on my face?
Masked all of my identifiables,
Alterations undeniable,
Can you hear me without judgment?
UNCLOUTHED in increments,
The impression is forming with a raw stream of curiosity,
Like the wind that blows,
You don't know it's full implicitly,
Implications of a woman scorned have taken place,
You'll never know,
Until you felt the EMOTIONS copywritten on my face,
Tasting the lasting imperfections,
Translucent societies,
gradual irritations,
Creations,
Of the most-high,
We don't question why,
Our soul SPEAKS in parables,
Purified intangibles,
Akashic records have my written my manuscript,
Observations of flows outwardly inn,
Intercepting fading out,

My emotions are venting,
Seeping,
The fuck out,
Tired of the boundary lines placed on me,
Feels like the wall is being built periodically,
AROUND me,
Chipping at it with a pickax,
It always builds back,
Because time creates movements around ME,
Without my permission,
They ground me,
All this massive ass gravity pulling me down,
Into quicksand,
I TRY not to drown,
Upon reflection,
The providing tones that I allow TO invade me,
My soul pulls me up from the mercy waters,
And SAVE ME,
No help from the bodies that invaded my space,
I'm the only one that can release me from this place.

EVEN

Piss on *YOUR* lips,
you couldn't hear me *EXHALE*,
I died in clear view of you,
EXHAUSTED and hurt,
Which you melted *MY* shin,
Call me a bitch,
Insinuating *SELF-WORTH*,
You degraded me,
Betrayed me,
Fucked me,
Traded me,
Only to leave hatred in my nucleus,
Including this,
I buried you all,
Only to have to relive it again,
Taking up too much *SPACE*,
If I could,
I *WOULD* castrate you all,
I have two fingers and a dildo on call,
I don't need boys at my beck and call,
Why yawl *KEEP* fucking with *ME*,
Am I that gullible to walk on,
You don't think of me,
WALKING in my shoes,
You can't step out of your own,

Fuck yawl in my consequential tone,
I'll be alright,
No matter yawl inconsistencies,
In due time,
I'll be able to dispose of you,
Cutting my skin to let yawl in,
Never again.

UNKNOWN

Blue velvet lines cross the dime lit skies,
Noctilucent clouds racing,
Crystalizing the impressions in our cortex,
Forming a cocktail for imagination,
Impressionable upon the mind,
Seeing past time,
Drifting through WORLDS unlike mine,
Discovering the secret meanings of numbers,
Symbolic expressions of colours,
Synergy in the writings of our ancestors,
Seeing the universe that LIVES INSIDE
of ourselves and others,
Fallen in love with the endless sensation,
One touch of kinetic motion that appears before the nation,
Balancing my natural instincts,
Feeling OF superior,
Not no more inferior,
My words will be heard,
MY senses are heightened,
More enlightened,
I'm your gatekeeper,
To help you keep your free verse,
Open your MIND,
Your heart,
Your spirit,
Your soul,
To the unknown,

Elevation can caress the imperfection,
that has been prolonged,
Darkness imbedded the sanctified of the
wiling temptation of negativity thereof,
Creation of our vessels,
Contracting the fabrication of
unsurpassable enlightenments,
We're living in a microenvironment,
Nothing is made,
Where everything is created.

UNHEALED WOUND

THE eyes tell a STORY,
YOU'LL HAVE to look closer TO SEE,
Peel back THE SURFACE,
THE separation is what you'll see OF me,
Continuous LIES,
Hurt that won't fade away,
Ignore THE PAIN,
Abuse that traumatized me,
Still to this very day,
I have encountered on my journey,
I bend to seek,
Lowering my head,
While my hands are raised high,
I pray to the most-high,
WANTING the answers,
Wanting to commit TO enhancers,
To end my life,
I cry,
I cry,
Feeling my blood pressure rise,
I HAVE stood alone,
Fighting the world on my own,
Settling for everything,
Never expecting,
THINGS to get better,
Sitting in quiet stillness,
Hoping the darkness will fade away,
I write my departure,

Seeing my rebirth
I feel betrayed,
Before and after,
Nowhere to turn but *TO* mother earth,
I finish my line,
Rehearse my verse,
Sitting on the edge,
I place the circle between the wedge,
Closed my eyes and didn't see my worth,
but hear my kids' verse,
Seeing them in my head,
I put down the lead,
The visions of my past have never stopped,
Will they ever *STOP*?

LACK OF

I,
Can't be viewed by someone who's not *EXPERIENCED* life,
Mindless distractions of fighting coherences,
Nothing can be done with the noise of loud cries,
Only the experienced *KNOWS* what the future lies,
So many ambitions untold and unset,
My heart wants my eyes wet,
Growing up without that leadership I truly deserved,
Now twenty-seven, I'm not *A FALLEN TREE*,
Entity goes on with the prospects of risk,
Life does not have instructions recorded,
on a flash drive or a disk.

LOST

Footsteps shift the textures of MY SUFFOCATION,
I'm unbalanced, unstructured, my body's been tortured,
Weighing of nothingness in my lost mind,
Altering my matrix,
Can my leveled thoughts IMPRINT WORDS on the lines?
Changing me TO the norm, which I am not,
Distorting my vallecular mythology,
Reflecting long intervals in gradual intermissions,
Transmitting sonic waves,
Physically affecting my soul on this planet,
Dripping cosmic verbiage vibrations,
Revolutionized characteristics,
Rejuvenating my lost,
SELF-ELEVATION.

HEAD GAMES

For the short time we had,
I loved THE ROAD I thought we would travel,
But as time went on, your valid light UNRAVELED,
The woman you once had with the children of two,
She always proclaimed that she was with you,
How CAN I compete with your past life of eight years?
The truth lied stuck in the back of my head,
but BECAME my biggest fears,
The feeling I have for you I never shared for no other,
I guess you looked at me like I was just your friend,
What was it about me that you didn't like?
Was it that I wasn't your type?
That I liked to compete without giving up a fight?
Or was it that I showed out the true me,
Not being fake and just being who I am,
Ever since you got out,
You showed you weren't the same,
You called every two days while playing the game,
Why wouldn't I think you weren't back with her?
I should have KNOWN,
You were wrapped around her pinky finger,
Shame on me for putting myself in that recycling bag,
Shame on me for thinking I can get back what I once had,
I'm getting older, and I can finally see,
That every man has a different impact on me.

A LETTER

I know when we first met, life for you *LOOK* so good,
A month later you got locked up because
of your love for the hood,
As time went on, we had gotten *CLOSER* to some degree,
Your past life took a toll *ON* us,
I liked a man I couldn't impact,
Until you found out you had a little girl which was a fact,
You changed *YOUR* life for the girl you always craved,
You could escape the formula that hindered your *LIFE*,
You took it out on everyone,
Including someone close to being your girl,
I had to step back and analyze our situation,
I didn't want you to feel that frustration,
Knowing I was out here without you by my side,
I tried to grow with you, but I needed to let you go,
I know it's messed up how you slowly up and left,
I guess you wanted to save me from myself,
Who wants to be locked up with their woman on the outside,
I know it was your concern, I heard it in your tone,
Your heart is so fragile, like a feather in the wind,
This is a letter to an inmate,
I hope I don't send.

A Moment

I fly over my image and view my reflection,
Watering me down till I evaporate,
Filtering my mind of past events,
Of what one man did to show his power,
For a while,
I HAD some bad moments that took
me to A different world,
No sanctuary
No sanity,
Took me out of this realm,
I'm writing for all to hear,
There's no HIDDEN MESSAGE,
I have confronted the man with the black-handled steal,
In my face,
To the side of my head,
I thought this nigga must be insane,
To put his finger on the chrome,
I stood with my back to the cold wall,
I told him to pull the trigger,
My body is tired,
As my thoughts progressed
You kicked me when I was 8 months distressed,
You use sex as a weapon,
Made me walk with my head hung low,
Humiliated me in front of your family for they all did know,
Dragging me across the floor with no one to help,
Gave me a black eye,
No doctors could save me,

Only to relieve me of an STD that you consistently gave me,
Feeling so alone,
Looking at this demand in my face,
Clench the trigger,
So I can be free,
He pushed me with the gun,
Then walked away,
My life hasn't even started,
My experiences have carved me,
Shaped me to fear man,
Developed me to have no life's plan,
Only to walk through life,
Fearing all men.

ENDURING

It has *NEVER* been denied that I care for you,
Even though there's a woman of two,
There's nothing I can do,
I'm doing bad *IN* the simple fact that my
emotions are wrapped into you,
MY EYES are numb,
My stomach hurts,
I'm humped on the floor,
Shivering and shaken,
But what the hell for,
You don't pay any rent in my mind,
To evict it,
I need to shift it,
I *HAVE* to let it go,
The stress,
To relieve,
I have to depress,
The memories in this realm,
The race,
The chase,
I have to have some space,
Forsaken the day I meet you,
Regretting the feelings that I went through,
Though I realized my time has come and gone,
I deprived myself for too damn long,
The lines that retract,
Seems to dissipate with time,
spray layers over hurt layers,

Building up the explosion,
Of the emotions,
Coating it with baby powder,
Eventually, it will blow off,
Is the only way to endure,
The cheating.

REMEMBER

When I'm alone,
I remember,
From when you slept with that girl in my house,
On my bed,
Where I rest my head,
When you got my car and credit card stolen,
My heart dropped,
My trust for you has been taken away long ago,
When you kept leaving for weeks,
Nowhere you could be found,
No proudness was in my eyes,
Lies,
Nothing but lies you told me,
Pregnant and depressed,
NONE the less,
Chasing you around town,
You OWNED me,
Infatuated my mind,
Collecting new negative energy that I can't delete,
Left you alone after that,
Still,
You came back,
Into an empty home,
With empty words,
You are dead to ME.

MY BROKEN FOCUS

IN A web of hard mistrust of reality,
I can't escape my caged mentality,
Chained away in the dry confusion,
Engaging every WOMAN'S illusion,
Timidly moving step by step,
Pulsating HEART beat as I wept,
Skin tingling from trying to break free,
Motionless,
Powerless,
IT'S A feel of me,
The saga never ends,
Of this HARD as reality from within,
Can't take the oxygen that's on my shoulders,
Damn,
The fucking world for passing me over,
I was homeless at a point in time,
A life paraded by crime,
A single parent,
With three sons in a compromising positing,
Why the hell couldn't I see this from
a mother's OBSERVATION,
That you wouldn't be there.

EXHAUSTED

I lost myself in your hopes and in your dream,
Flourishing in the MOMENTS only to relinquish me,
Slowly leaving our routine in the past,
Reassuring,
Understanding,
Compromising of the hand,
Not knowing what the next day brings,
EXHAUSTED by the momentum of your passion,
You left me in the ripple,
Only to cater to everyone else,
I sit patiently by myself,
Texting,
Social media has replaced MY time,
My MIND,
Can't unwind,
Waiting to see if things will change,
Waiting to see if you need me the same,
Where is the man I once knew?
Wrapped up in the future moments,
Who knew,
You would change for the sake of fame,
Drinking my glory way,
I take my mind away,
Covering me with the past of what was,
Taking the time to acknowledges my sadness,
Nurturing my unhappiness,
When will it go back to when it was?
When will it go back to how we loved?

THE DREAM

So lost in the thought,
  The thought of being more,
Being more than what I am,
  A nameless NOBODy,
A nobody without a name,
  A name without a face,
A faceless slab of skin,
  Just taking up space,
I'm just one person,
  Trying to make it,
Trying to be known,
  In the space that I invade,
Conflicted in the image,
  That society holds to be true,
To be true is a perception,
  Your perception known to you.

MEMORY BOX

The night has *FALLEN* into a black hole,
Alone again with only strangers' voices unknown,
Lights glare past me to race for their moment of *SOLITUDE*,
Once my mind is at rest,
The thought rise from the dead,
Again, alone with no one to glance at,
The sky filled with colors,
AGAIN, damn again,
Is the fifteen-minute light show not worth anyone's time,
Past keeps creeping up,
Slowing,
Filling the lines of the body with emptiness,
Tears run,
Trying to swallow,
Fuck it,
ANOTHER year,
Holiday *PAST*,
Another *MARK* under the belt in the memory box.

Ma'at the Poet

·CHAPTER TWO·

AM I ENOUGH FOR THOSE WHO I
THOUGHT MATTERED?

WORDS TO SOON

What PEOPLE say to get their feelings aroused,
Not to mislead or throw them off,
I said something that I shouldn't have said,
Deep emotions can get you in TROUBLE
that you couldn't imagine,
When your heart feels that nonnegotiating passion,
Abandonment,
Confusion,
My heart cries within,
Mind filtered of what could have been,
Thoughts of him render my focus,
Making me feel like a locus,
Draining ME of my sense of leisure,
Damn near feel like I'm about to have a seizure,
I want this man out of my head,
I wish for those feelings went unsaid,
He left me because of what I said,
What people say to get their feelings across,
Not to mislead or throw them off,
Truth.

MOMENT OF ALTERED VALUE

When I see you,
I don't see what could be,
I see what could have been.
My lens of you have been adulterated,
INFECTING my mind to revert back in time,
COMPLEXING on self-value,
Not enough,
I'm so not tough,
Speak to me,
Mirror,
Mirror on the wall,
What do you see when you look back at me?
Can you see me at all?
An empty reflection with no on there,
Translucent at best,
I'm broken in silence not for all to see,
Irreversible pain,
UNBALANCED at my feet,
Miss placed by shattered glass,
Unrepairable at the edges,
Holding tight the solid prism of self,
Trying to let go of the cuts that kept me bleeding,
Tapping to soothe,
Crying for self-comfort,
Align my SPIRIT with the stars,
Fall when God calls me home,
But only then will I fall.

PROGRESS

I'm fed up with wanting,
To wanting to be happy,
In the most prominent TIME in my life,
My spirit filled with musical notes,
But my eyes experienced past inconsistencies OF harmony,
Putting up my defenses so I,
Can protect the shallow waters,
Riding the tides, ACKNOWLEDGING the
lies, distinguishing man from mortars,
My cries,
Inflame the dirty shame that my voice won't make a sound,
Connecting the others that came from my mother,
The cycle seems to be rotating, repeating,
and recycling irrational thinking,
Song in progress, melody not heard,
emptiness is its own reward,
I know this sound; don't think I'm going
insane; it's just one of my CONDITIONS,
Nervousness circles the sparkle of minutes
that TANGLES by the hours,
Synthetic gestures swinging side by side
dragging the hand of power,
The rhythm of plays forces me to rebound,
step back and lock through the center,
Catching one's personal worth in the
reflection that I can enter,

I'm glad I am the way I am to make
my BLACK generation proud,
I'm going to alter the notes that fell off the page,
And try to create a whole,
That they laid.

PURE INTENTIONS

You,
The tone of your abundance delivered in your vibrations,
Draping your dialogue to fit your situations,
And I, am selfish.

You,
Sound your kingdom out in translucent clarity as a prism,
Scattered footprints of your weakness
of abstract expressionism,
And I, am not wearing a mask.

You,
Throw your words on creativity while
knowing your egotistical aroma,
Enticements on the statuettes creating tainted villoma,
And I, am not going in circles.

You,
You bind me with your I am King,
Do as I say, don't do as I do,
Running from something that is right in front of you,
And I, am pure intentions.

INSTALL

So many thoughts,
So many tears,
So many frustrations,
Over so many years,
Rows of regrets,
Times I felt threats,
Lies and deception,
Gray manipulation,
Headaches and heartbreak,
So many so fake,
Everything and everyone ISN'T WHAT things seems,
I don't live in reality,
I live in my daydreams,
Caress me,
Heal me,
Want me,
Love me,
Spiritually connect with me,
Be my friend,
Can't you see I'm on edge,
That cheating shit,
You can take to someone else's bed,
Stop introducing that to my life,
Before I slash one of you with this sharp ass knife,
Why can't you handle or understand?
What I want is a true real man.

IN NEED

I pace my steps to clear my mind,
Feeling the intertwine of the carpet between my toes,
Running my fingers aside the walls,
Hearing my nails scraping the paint,
The same worries and the same debates,
My soul seems to not comprehend,
God help me,
Please help.

I DON'T WANT TO BE YOU

I see you shifting unannounced to you,
I see you,
Hiding behind the fog,
The light is turned on in my eyes,
I see the wrong,
Masking your sadness,
I can hear your tone,
Underneath that smile,
I see the branches that got you years of dead leaves,
Just clinging on for dear life because
he's all you have known,
Paralyzed by the lies and secrets that were untold,
Collapsing your heart to harden and parting your intuition,
Excepting what you can't change,
I don't want to be you,
Hearing late night steps,
Vibrations of silence through the air,
Heartbeat pulsating fast,
Tears you thought won't last,
Mind won't stop the assumptions,
Interruptions,
From your mental instability,
Changing you,
To see things you thought wasn't true,
I hear he's just like his dad,
Echo's through my soul,
His DNA is strong,
He's his father's son,

I sit and think,
Will that be the vision of me?
Bitter with hostility,
Limited liability,
To your capabilities,
Filling the space of numbers within time,
Walking that thin line,
Insanity or jeopardy,
I chose neither,
Putting up with the blisters that he wouldn't,
Emotions that he couldn't,
Cheating which he shouldn't,
Yet,
You do,
I don't want to walk in your shoes,
But every step I take,
I feel as though I'm getting closer to you,
Your image of sad stories played in a song,
Infatuating your senses.
The ice crystals fall from the sky,
Trembling beneath your world,
Clotting your vessel,
Feeling perishable,
I can't be you,
I can't be you,
Longing for the day the fog will go away,
Only to say,
These words one day,
I am not you.

MY DRIVE

Damn, I got to punch the clock,
I don't want to go to work today,
Got to get dressed,
Got to fight this traffic,
Cussing everybody out in some way,
In my mind,
Got to drive behind these slow ass people
that shouldn't be on the road,
Push the brakes every 20 seconds
because of they so damn old,
Then you got the ones that can't stay in their fucking lanes,
Causing traffic to slow down,
Damn this shits a pain,
You do 70 in a 55 but they still on your ass,
See, I slow down to piss them off,
Then look at them when they pass,
I cranked up my sounds to get motivated for this damn day,
I see my job,
Man,
This is going be a hell of a fucked-up day.

GROWTH AND DEVELOPMENT

Venture into the forest of my soul,
You chopped down my virtue to the root,
Raindrops of leaves carpets my bark,
Why does the air have to be so thin in my world?
Why look at me and make me feel rotted?
My days are embarking on a cold heart,
Ignore the hazel glare and the cracked branches,
Ignore the brown leaves that dangle,
But don't look at me as if you want to clime me,
Look at me as something beautiful,
Graceful,
Valued,
Adored by nature,
Don't chop me down,
Don't put me into the fire,
In time I will grow,
Mature,
See the world in a new light,
Explode with radiance,
I just need time,
For me to show you my worth.
I'm like a child,
Very impressionable,
But sensational,
I pick up on your creativity,
Playing my symphony,
On the playground,
I'm free like the wind,

Going in all directions,
Chiming in,
Through enlightenment,
you will see me,
Who am I?
I am the light that can't be controlled,
I am the electricity that is not grounded,
I am the water that satisfies your thrust,
Many of souls,
One mind,
Plenty of spirits,
Developed over time,
Rewinding to go back to the beginning,
When all things,
Were,
Just all things,
I'm noticeable because I'm me,
I'm a seed because I'm still changing,
One body,
Many impressions,
The infancy of my universe,
One continuous thought,
Who am I?
Multiple illusions of dreams,
Declaring my enoughness,
Vulnerable to humans,
I am a product of my Kings,
That was not Kings,
Unrevealing creaked doors,
Speaking my mind only to myself,
Do you really know me?
Behind my eyes,

In the regression of self,
I am not my outer being,
I'm free like a rebirth,
In my inner dwelling,
You genuinely don't see me,
Who am I?
I'm a procrastinator for the things I want?
I help people get the things they need?
Forgetting about myself,
My emotions,
Thoughts,
Feelings,
Impressions,
Forgetting me,
What am I?
I am not your friend,
I have a more profound gravity than titles,
Sh'khinah Ma'at Sophia Yisreal,
I'm beyond this universe,
A deep rethinker,
A spiritual being,
I am Queen,
Don't make me something I'm not,
I am what I am,
Sometimes I'm misunderstood,
verbally,
mentally,
sexually,
I overstand,
I chose not to be dialogued,
Defaulted into your scenario of lust,
You may have raped my physical,

Body,
View,
Traces of safeness,
The Kilomole,
Perception and sensation of my soul,
Will always be,
What I am not,
Is your Bitch,
Your chick,
Your angry black woman,
See me beyond the physical image of your lens,
Let me,
Impregnate your cerebral cortex,
Center me at your higher thought process,
Touching your center lob with impulse control,
Let me,
Meditate on your amygdala,
While studying the Kabballah,
Can you reach 125 degrees?
Reaching the full spiritual enlightenment,
Connecting with your spiritual being for incitement,
The music of our ancestors,
Who am I,
The one who is creating creativity,
Simplicity,
The overstanding of the inner mist of me,
Do you see me now?
As I write the sounds,
Of my rhythmic tones,
Phalanges banging to release your wrongs,
Feeling a sense of freedom that's really not free,
But I'm just giving you a layer of me,

Again,
Who am I?
Who am I?
I am.
I am.
I am that I am.

SHADOWS

I remember back in the days when I
had no money to feed my kids,
I remember when the roaches acted as
if they were our best friends,
I looked back on plenty of times where
I couldn't pay my bills,
Plenty of nights of cold, dark days
where my mind chased hills,
Why did we have it so hard?
My oldest son had asked me?
I just walked away,
Cried,
Left things the way they are,
I confided in God to help his child in need,
I asked God to help plant hissed,
But as time went on things got harder,
In the dim of the night,
I have gotten stronger,
He helped me see.

SCHOOL

Here it is at 6 o'clock am,
Got to get up for school,
I'm dragging tail,
But I got to haul ass,
What Am I gonna do?
Put in gym class heroes to get me in the right mood,
Listening to Travis dancing in the mirror, oh,
I'm running out of time,
Find an inspirational outfit that fits my physic,
Not everybody can wear,
Not to be a critic,
I slip on my k-swiss,
I'm out the door,
Oh I forgot my bookbag,
Never mind,
What I need that for,
I hum cupid's chokehold till 5th period,
Dreaming about meeting Travis,
The bell rings,
Then it ended,
The day went long,
Eventually ended,
Walked back home where I resented
To the feng shui of my room,
Adding my EARBuDS to extinguish tomorrow.

NOT JUST WORDS

Deliberately thinking,
Metaphorically speaking,
I walk with a curve,
Structurally superb,
The way I am,
Interacts with my speaking,
Intellect so engraved,
My senses concaved,
If you read my lips,
See what I've heard,
My fenced in world rotates,
Smack your lips,
You'll taste chicken and beans,
Don't try to perceive what you see and hear of me,
My vibe is surpassed your degree.

WAIT, WHAT?

You're trying to confuse me,
With your over the top, put together alphabet?
Wanting me to read between the lines,
While paraphrasing your actions,
Living a second life on borrowed time,
Unplug the stair master of paganism,
With your pre-loaded skills having fun,
As I sit here and wait on you to justify me,
Holding you up on the chapters of your life,
Wear the shoe that fits, I guess,
Love is not going to follow me as I try to read you,
Looking in my rear view,
At you,
Disgusting as you try to make me understand,
You bastard,
I'm not a board game to strategize,
To emphasize your side chicks,
You are the bitch,
Hardening my emotions,
Stirring up commotions,
Inside of me,
See you in passing.

IT

Bam, it hits you like an oncoming train,
Your feelings, your wants, your dreams,
your centrifuge is all the same,
Wrapped up in one bundle of incredible
taste that's not tamed,
All you think about,
All you crave,
Can never allude you,
Not knowing the feelings is growing fast and out of control,
Putting it all together,
You grow as a whole,
Is it lust,
Infatuation,
If not,
Then what is it,
The deep-down gradual consumption enhances your soul,
Staring into the secrets mind,
Consoling,
The addiction of love,
It's so amazing,
When it's with the right person that's loving you back too.

JUST FOR ME

I tell myself everything will be alright,
But I know the truth,
I'm not going to worry about any man,
I'm going to focus on me and close the door,
Over you,
It's not going to happen,
Distorted tempered,
It's not going to dampen,
The reality of my day
Locked in every which way,
Sentenced to be heard,
Loved, touched, held, and in every word,
I'm going to lay back, chill, and let my mind loose,
Put on some John Tesh,
Let my surrounding be contused,
I can't help but say,
It feels good to be about me,
Exhaling my mind,
Thinking about me for the first time.

FOR THOSE ON THE OUTSIDE

If you stand before God would you
be able to confess your sins,
When you lay your head down at night
could you close your eyes at the end,
If someone told you wouldn't make it,
Would you let go or hold on within,
When you go out and stand up on your own,
What impression would you send?
If someone talked bad of you showing fake
love as if they were your friend,
Acting as if they'll be there for you till the very end,
When someone shatters your heart in
places that you can't mend,
Will you be able to give different faces
without traces of pretend?
I don't feel bad for the person on the outside looking in,
I'm just glad they aren't going through
what I'm going through deep in sin.

THE OTHER SIDE

Where am I, it's dark, I can't find my way,
I'm scared of being alone, I don't want to stay,
Who is in here with me, nothings around me, but fear,
I feel cold, I feel warm, I'm confused, why am I here,
Empty space, can I even ignore what's going on,
consciousness,
Is what I see really what I see,
Is the darkness a reality?
Am I in the light, so bright that it's distorting my vision,
I can't see hands,
Am I standing,
I can't hear, feel, or see anything beneath me,
Am I walking, sitting, am I floating in midair,
I want to scream, can I scream, my
mouth is numb, is it there,
I'm alone, so alone, is there anyone else here,
Can it be that I'm going insane?
In a subconscious state that I can't adhere,
Is it me that's thinking these words,
How can I believe if everything around me is not before me?
Can I even be here, is myself being deprived form of reality,
The void is getting longer, is anyone there,
Is this a dream, can someone help me,
I want to leave this place?

Out of the unknown is a radiant light,
With the faint soothing breeze,
At that moment, I realize,
From the opening of the sight,
A bright light,
I'm dead.

AT PLAY

Setting at the park watching all the innocence,
No bills, no traffic tickets, play in its persistence,
No worrying about men or women
trying to steal their time,
No fears of unfaithful people trying to undermine,
They climbing the monkey bars, racing down the slide,
Playing tag,
Other kids charging about who lied,
Gossiping teen girls standing with their crew,
While the boys are checking them out,
Only if they knew,
Little kids in the sandbox building castles with their hands,
Having all these dreams,
Letting them play out in the sand,
No worries, no cares just kids at play,
One day when they grow up,
They will be thinking this same very way.

DREAM

I'm going to let the wind take me away,
From all this fake nonsense,
Interrupting my fictitious dream,
Let me be,
Just for a second,
Let me dream,
Just for a second,
Just want to dream,
It don't have to be real,
It doesn't have to be 3d,
I wish to be left alone with my thoughts of what could be.

COVERING BLACK

I need a moment of clarity, to inspect my inner being,
Replenishes my mindset, and unbox a light that's gleaming,
I'm writing this to unleash some tension,
of a black woman's distress,
Excuse me if I get to raspy and step out of dress,
I'm a 22-year-old woman that has had my share of drama,
Why everybody gets to hate on me
because they hate their momma,
Smile, talk bad about you in a minute,
lies right out bluntly in your face,
Niggas get mad, call me out my name,
I don't want to give you my flower,
Look, my guy, don't take it the wrong way
but I don't get paid by the hour,
I'm strong willed, open minded, and
in depended black warrior,
Hazel eyes, caramel complexion, and take it as I want it,
Don't get it twisted, I'm unique in stature,
Similarities with another don't exist,
Take it to mind, I'm a single black woman
with features that you can't miss,
Underneath it all, I got to be me,
Unique in stature, that's how it's gonna be.

NEGOTIATING FREEDOM

Editing my face to look presentable to
societies known to normality,
Caged in the frontal lobe of my mind
trying to breathe life into me,
Pushing pause on my visions only to keep tracing my image,
Sunken insecurities that have been
carved from my past by man,
Reflection mirrors can't show,
The truth inside the masked face that I bestow,
My gaze is faced at the abyss,
You would never distinguish the writings on my retinas,
The agony that is fertilized into my playbook of scenes,
Acting the part of the eyes unseen,
Formulating my cortex to see geometric forms,
Venting my pathways to shape the collection of thoughts,
A speckle of light flashes in front of my eyelids closed,
Seeing the imperfections that my
mind thinks everyone knows,
Clothing my body of souls that are not of my own,
Trying to be someone,
That isn't me,
Understanding the numbers that are given to me at birth,
Relating to the Stockholm syndrome That
the aliens that gave me my worth,
Idealized what you think you see,

You don't know the half of what this
world has shipped to me.
I can't be free from these designated
drivers with false identities,
So, I wait,
So, I wait,
Continuously negotiating my freedom as it comes.

NEGOTIATING FREEDOM PART 2

When I think,
I'm over all that has happened,
You remind me every day of how vulnerable I am,
Shackled to your demands,
I can't move past the lies that withstands,
The motionless time that I see around me,
You remind me,
Of how time repeats,
Which never sleeps,
On my watch,
I'm awaken,
You mistaken,
The counterfeit hands of time,
Which you replicate,
While another sit still and wait,
You can't eject the triggers that a line my parietal lob,
America,
I am not fooled.

HOMEGIRL

They saw me as that girl,
  That homegirl that's a pearl,
    Fascinating to know a girl as I,
    That tomboy,
However, I was viewed as their toy.

They see me as that girl,
  Playing ball in the streets,
    Wrestling in the yard was a treat,
    Imagine me,
But, yawl don't see the real girl.

The cute girl down the street,
  Wearing boy clothing to cover,
    The thickness of my selfless insecure curvatures,
    Vulnerability as,
Also, the endless tone of the unknown,

They saw me with their ideology,
  Their lips ignored my name,
    I will always be just that girl,
    Always ashamed,
Furthermore, that girl that's unknown to name.

Ma'at the Poet

•CHAPTER THREE•

REFLECTING ON THE CONSPIRACY
THAT I HAVE WITHIN MYSELF

NOTHING ELSE

I walk, with a glide, of an awakening of my pride,
with you by my side I will always rise,
I am wanted with no fear, of cheating or
disparities, I grew into clarity,
Step forth into faith, as I stay in his grace,
separate your head from your heart,
I dully depart, macro cognoscenti, transparent
and illuminating joy within me,
I will always be your wife,
As you breathe,
I breathe life.

THE RESIDUE

Feeling burnt out incandescent when you're not here,
The space is empty,
My thoughts are so unclear,
Feeling the pressure of the roof falling in,
Needing you….
The whole has become visible to my senses,
Smelling your scent on the pillows,
Feeling your touch on my skin,
Hearing your tone in the sounds you make,
Needing you…
Feeling so lost,
Like a lost puppy,
Been only an hour,
However; seems like forever,
Please hurry back home.

GROWING WITHIN

As you connect with me,
feel the light that's radiating intensity,
empathy,
upon my vulnerability,
I feel blessed but worthless,
agitative complexity,
fenced in aggressively,
wanting to scream,
but,
you can't see me,
prolonging my agony,
dwelling inside of me,
I feel a rage,
decomposing myself,
an angry black woman is what I would be cited,
recall,
I said no,
but you didn't hear me,
I said stop,
you said fuck me,
I told you it hurts,
you said kill yourself,
as I clutch in agony,
invisible as I lay as your pray,
your intentions were already in play,
non-negotiating the light that is
illuminating from within me,
you don't see,

Queen,
you see infancy,
delinquency in the not knowing,
calculating the foundation,
you planted inside me,
exploding out,
A quiet storm,
lay doormat,
I died,
The seed has been planted,
not enough,
unviable,
recyclable,
Digestible,
only fuckable,
you,
see me,
You don't see shit,
Moving forward,
I disappeared from your world,
I excavated my universe,
Replacing it with,
That I am,
rebirth,
of a Queen.

NEAR YOU AGAIN

I close my eyes,
As I lay in bed with you,
I pray second by second that this will be true,
I don't ever want this night to be through,
I can't help to imagine,
Kissing you all through the night,
As I lay in bed with you,
What's the vision that's going on in your head?
Could you be thinking of what I said?
Vibrating sensations, throbbing heat,
You are one of your own among the elite,
As I lay in bed with you,
Are legs crossing touching one another?
Licking my lips in such wonder,
Your lips look delicious to my curious eye,
Feeling your hand, placing on my thigh,
Underneath the cover and never questioning why,
As I lay in bed with you, embracing
every minute of the time,
Wanting you to be totally mine,
Recognizing what kind of King you are,
Passionate, unique, and real, you are,
As I lay in bed with you, the vibe that
I receive from your presents,
I crave your very essence,
The shine that comes from your heart,
It distinguishes you way apart,
As I lay in bed with you,

I Adorn your body that's pressed against my skin,
Holding back the temptation that fights from within,
Wanting so much to feel you and breath you,
Bath in your voice,
I want it to be my choice,
As your locs lay across the pillow like writings in a book,
My mind wonders what they would feel,
Like across my flowing brook,
Your natural scene is illuminating,
Hoping you're feeling the same way that I'm engaging,
Undeniable throbbing,
I'm not going to justify the feelings with sex,
Not to be in the wrong context,
I want to be one with you,
But for now,
Can we just lay here for a while?
Can we just lay here for a while?
When I open my eyes,
You're not here,
Feeling so real,
The phone rings,
Press 5.
Hi baby, I just had a dream about you, man.
Thank you for calling. I can't wait to make
love to you in the physical. I miss you.

CHANGE

The deeper I fall for you, the louder I call for you,
Unsound thoughts wrapping my cognizance,
Reasoning about my providence,
Where we were, we are now,
I write, lowing my brow,
seeing images of my husband's vow,
I cry for you,
As your light comes through,
This mist of a world,
Contour that I am,
Seeing you as you are, and would remain,
Branching out to explore your type of endearment,
Your kind of love makes me feel fearless.

AS WE ARE

As we talked,
I looked deep into your eyes,
Passionate suggestions flow through my mind,
I rubbed my fingers through your hair,
I slowly learn your unique ways,
As we talked,
Your words gave me ravish thrills,
My stomach experienced such good chills,
I projected us as one,
I felt what was imbedded into your soul,
As we talked,
I couldn't help but to stair,
Even if it was a glare,
You felt what I felt when the feeling is so real,
The design of recognition among sex appeal,
Antonym's and metaphors paraphrased your words,
The gesture of your accent is something to be heard,
As we talked,
You took me to a natural addition,
My heart was pounding with such affection,
Boy, what are you doing to me?
I felt the colours of the soul from a distend land,
Repetitive motions,
Crystal blue oceans,
I felt the breeze,
The silence is at ease,
The trees were dancing to the wind's melody,
My body, mind, and soul felt it so slowly,

As we talked,
freelancing the words that came to me,
Not thinking of the complexity,
Wanting you to touch me,
Nothing but me,
Wanting you to see me,
Nothing but the true me,
I want you to hear me,
If nothing else,
Just for you to see me,
Listen to my heart's plea.

TO THE PAST – THAT LITTLE GIRL

You had nothing but yourself to look upon,
In a lonely chaotic basement that you called your home,
Scuffed with your belongings that did not resemble you,
Dusty memories lay on the walls of suppressed eyes lids,
Counterintuitive to internal review,
You had no one that could say they understood you,
So, you wet your chapter,
Contrasted into paper,
Looking outside the thick plated glass windows,
Wiping the cobwebs from the observation
that created shadows,
Behind others,
You stand,
Shy as a bird hiding in her nest,
Clinging to her mother's breast,
In the basement you stand alone,
Covered with the things that are well known,
Blanked by comfort,
As you remained,
Misunderstood.

GRATEFUL

I'm addicted to a man's touch,
My body so responsive and surreal,
His tongue moistening my neck with such raw appeal,
His hands feel like medicine to my body
Nurturing me,
Healing my soul,
With one look in his eyes,
I get so nervous,
Losing myself in focus,
Methodically caring for my body,
He took me to a place of utmost satisfaction,
Could it be that it's been a while for me,
Something that I needed that I never got from my past,
I don't care, I want this feeling to last,
I'm an addict of a man's touch,
It is so raw and delightful,
His breathe along my back makes everything
else seems so less meaningful,
Gentile kisses to the back of my thighs,
Sending my heartbeat to a maximum high,
Invigorating, animating, exhilarating, and aggressive,
His virile is virtuous uttering things in perspective,
Visions of this, I thought could never happen,
This man brings a whole new meaning
of sensual satisfaction,
A dream is all it was, of a man that I have met,
A dream, in reality, I hope it will project.

I HAVE ANOTHER LOVE

My heart is open to you,
As I lay down the welcome mat,
I see I love another,
Is it true,
That I can be in love with two,
Feeling the twitter in my stomach,
As I see both of you,
Loving you both in different ways,
My body is filled with inspiration,
So much stimulation,
That my clitoris feels as you both penetrate,
My soul to hydrate,
All of me,
Working together to channel,
What I never knew was in me,
One helped to understand how I can love,
The other,
Is me.

BEHIND CLOSED DOORS

The colour of time which passes by with every Second,
I'm grasping the very essence of his
breath that He breaths in me,
The dew from his lips wrap around
mine to Interlock us as one,
Layering thoughts stepped pass my contort reason,
Portraying to hold back the live wire,
Shifting my passion to stop, but want more,
Wild lined aggression, rest on the crave of maximum high,
A bead of sweat down our skin,
Heat forms a mist on the windows pane,
After all, is said and done,
I get up,
Wink my eye,
And walk out the door.

BREATHE

My synergy is low,
Emotions are high,
I can't plant myself in stillness,
My foundation is crumbling,
Where's my self-worth,
Where's my light,
My identity has been draped over,
Clashing with madness,
I need to write my feeling out,
I need to scream and shout,
Let it all out,
And BREATHE.

SERENITY

Drifting by on a ray of light,
Relaxing fragments of healing,
Mythological reflection intercepting ones being,
Triumphant beams running through the inner seams,
Peacefully painting a handprint in the air,
Parallel converted line,
But who really care,
Open up to a world that embraces your unique genre,
Reveal what you have wanted to unleash and unhide,
Within to fly,
Spread your wings like a butterfly,
A shape of consciousness mystifying the illusion,
Coordinating the winds to not feel exclusion,
Quietly revealing what has been crashing inside,
Breath the BREATHE, that expels you,
Makes you,
Lives you, feel the glide,
Alone taking vigorous times in thought,
Settling in the tranquility of thought,
Flouting by on a ray of light,
Engaging in a fruitful flight,
Have serenity in your own breath of air,
Taking in every bit until you can't bear,
Uphold simulating blows that touche your skin,
Feeling of sleepiness that contends,
A peaceful flight is what I instill,
Daydream,
Let it take you away from here.

ETHEREAL

So soft and intricate to the senses of perception,
Infuse the chakra that is aligned with my interception,
Open my DNA to transmute the energy
of alignment with the universe,
transverse,
the diligent fringes that connect the path
to my mate as we integrate,
adjust my exhaling and inhaling to a slow pace,
Breath into me,
as I exhale into you,
Tantrum sex is what you about learn to do,
Joining the evolved on a sexual high that's
deeper than an exploding cum,
An inner orgasmic reception dissent from,
The teachings of our ancestors to reach the holistic orgasm,
As we elevate our sexual experience,
Crystalize as you spread apart the labia majora,
Feeling the balance as you get to the labia minora,
The vibration is activating the pullback of the clitoral hood,
Feeling the breeze and the hardness of the raw wood,
Gravitating to the aura,
Bringing me to the truth of spiritual ethereal,
Etherical,
Traveling under impressions of our ancestors,
Therapeutic harmonious sessions of transcendence,
Relax as the feeling of electricity extends its hand,
to your pineal gland,
reawakening the celerity,

feeling the clarity,
of my lotus flower within,
let it cum to you,
intense as it may,
leaking from your eyes,
the intensity of the feeling you going inside of me,
assisters come to you as you reach your crown,
glorifying life that's an endless bound,
cry into the emotions that your body is emphasizing,
While you go inside of me,
don't lie to me,
antagonizing me,
chime your frequency,
no negativity,
as you move mountains inside of me,
growing fiercely,
exult me as I look you in your eyes,
as I justify my moans as I cry,
ready to be accepted into this world,
the indigo blue,
parting the sea within my thighs shines true,
suctioning your shaft with my walls of life,
crystalizing you,
deepening into me,
I see inside of you,
connecting our DNA,
rejuvenating our genome,
synchronizing our carbon,
there's no bargain,
dig into me,
as I rotate closer to you,
creating a mind and body connection,

synergizing my body's orgasmic collaboration,
slowly feeling gratifying sensation,
wrapping my arms around you,
tighter,
deeper I look into you,
and we both,
I release.

UNSTABLE WATERS

My mind is potential kinetic energy
formulating its own vortex,
Illuminating the energy from the light
that my muscles put into motion,
I want to explore the gravitational pull,
yet,
The background noise keeps taking up my mental space,
Let my mind rest,
And digest,
For clarity,
With my polarity,
I'm continually constructing creative molarity,
Engaging my crystals so I can meditate,
I filter my thoughts through my hand,
Like sand,
They land,
Swell as the knowledge absorbs and creates energy,
Spherically,
Peace renders the static that surrounds me,
Electrifying My astrophysics inside of biology,
The atmospheric motion that embodies my grounding,
Is an owner's manual to my center,
Don't you dare enter,
This is my universe,
Let me Breathe,
Without any conceptualizing,
Manipulating,
Hydrolyzing,

Don't bring in your reality into my background noise,
Let me ingest the vibrations of my concentrated resonance,
My cells detangle as my high electromagnetic wave,
Synchronize with my imbalanced harmonic equilibrium,
don't fuck with my calm,
my synergy is ethereal,
Pending my rest,
I stress,
Tying to heal my emotional wounds,
Continuing to meet my disposition,
Retested,
Over time I will shatter,
There will be no laughter,
Building my Anahata from the ground up,
Repeatedly revisiting my prism,
Flocculating my mind to pronounce,
My calm.

TIME

Through a measure of time,
You'll be able to research my mind,
Never to understand,
The strategic moves I see far ahead or behind,
Surpassing time,
I may not be able to explain my reasons or whys,
Counting back the words of time,
My cells generate organized crime,
The world sees it as pantomime,
Looking through the rumination of my lens,
I'm innocent until proven guilty,
So they say,
I leave impressions of me along the way,
As a stray,
They can track me where I lay,
Imbedding my journey into their senses,
Screwing them tight so that time condenses,
To my will,
Illumination,
Changing the present time,
The past and future is a deficiency,
Through the measure of time,
you won't be able to research my mind,
you need a warrant to enter,
and still,
is time real.

COGNITIVE

Open my spiritual mind,
Explore with me,
Walk with me,
Talk with me,
Show me,
Gravitational empathy that unshaped me,
Using a powerful clay that made me,
Built my foundation up,
Only to make my structure unsound,
As you walk with me,
You break me down,
Flexing my emotions through gravitational law,
Contorting my fortitude and mind,
Refining my thinking not to be mine,
Exposed my travels to the galaxy that
I exponentially enhanced,
Travelling through dark matter, I see the light,
Reflecting back at me,
I am the light,
As I walk with me, talk with me, and take this ride,
I explore me, transvers me, then finally
I See the reasoning of my mind.

SPOKEN THROUGH INK

I lose myself in the verses I write,
Only to relive my untamed mortality,
To justify my place within my spirituality,
Moving at a pace that is my chosen,
Knowing my fate,
The taste of decay,
Risking it all for the moment for Zen and serenity,
I feel as if I'm losing my identity,
I have to rethink,
By tracing my every breath in ink,
It's always something to the thought,
Not knowing the dirty secrets that are
generated through my DNA,
Look into my x-ray,
My genetic heredity is traced from my untold past,
My ancestors are the original verbs,
I'm a victim of my words,
What is it to write with this hand that
holds a small piece of space,
This pen full of ink is the life force for unspoken thoughts,
Trapped in the darkness of un-birthed connections,
If I don't write,
What is to be read,
You would think there's nothing to be spoken of,
A void of synchronized static,
The soil of achromatic,
Emphatic soundwaves,
You'll miss it,

If you don't *see me*,
Unknown to *the unwoven*,
The page is full of context,
My thoughts are clear,
You have to hear me deeper and fully hear me,
Misread by some who don't understand me,
I'm reveling the *mysteries of my ink*,
So you and I can resume *my verse* to be sung,
Diverse to the touch,
Embraced by the smell,
Seen by the ear,
Complex,
I know,
To understand it's *to voice* the words being read,
Step into *my world* of the unbalanced,
The people are invalid,
Dated to the mist of the *conscious voice*,
Fenced in by a world of negative energy,
So I create a chemistry of *synergy in my bubble*,
Generating humbleness,
As I write tone,
Hear my ink,
As I am,
That I am.

CHANGED

Ignore me not,
*   For I am a powerful Hebrew woman,*
Rippling in the echoes of your cortex,
*   Imbedded in your Deoxyribonucleic acid,*
Channeling your molecules to replicate,
*   You try to defecate,*
On me,
*   I am not an afterthought,*
To pass one hit wonders on,
*   See me for the woman I am.*

CIRCADIAN RHYTHM

As time shift from night shift from day
and from the day to night,
Our hypothalamus decodes our inner minds state,
Collapsing our lids to be wakened with secretions of fluids,
Draining from our meibomian gland is our circadian lucid,
Shaping the fluctuations that revise our galaxy,
Limited to what we can't see,
Explore the size of your limitations in
our excretable universe intensely,
There's no end to our absorptions that are limitless,
Curve your universe to never be parallel to others,
The higher your primordiality,
People will follow one after another,
Don't disrupt your cycle that will put you in benightment,
The darkness in an organism's environment
that will not get you to free movement,
The matter of energy should be vast in its vibrations,
Enhancement,
enchantment,
Show me the light that you travelled through,
Show me the shape of the universe that's inside of you,
The cosmic mass that's invisible to others,
Tape into a suprachiasmatic nucleus
that will help you see further,
Fix your bedrock of understanding,
Giving your sleep is a pattern of rebirth,
Awakening of grandstanding.

DON'T BLINK

Hair dripping,
Muscles glistening,
How I would love to rub your body,
Feel every line that your body forms.
Climb on top of you, let my hands just feel you,
Close your eyes, and don't see.
Don't look, no view, just feel me,
As I verbalize your body,
Putting exclamation marks on every structure,
As I document where your body flinches of the
touch of me,
I'm looking, watching your every motion.
Seeing your lips how they move,
How they jester,
I lean forward to feel your breath on my lips,
While my breast touches your chest, I rotate my hips.
Your eyes still closed as I rub my hands down your limbs,
Touch your hands, locking fingers, I kiss on the rim,
Of your mouth,
Soft kisses, not hard, while I suck on your bottom lip,
I kiss your eyes and tell you to keep them closed,
As I continue to my lecture of your body,
rotate my hips,
Arching my back,
Rubbing forward with this kitty on your juicy dick,
Not to quicken our moment,
I slow down just a bit,
To hear you say I love you,

I sit up to rise
Put your hands on my thighs,
Move them to my ass,
Where you can get a grip that will last,
I lean back down and trace your ears with my tongue,
I feel your lungs...
Expand as I move to your neck,
Licking the beads of dips that wept,
I tell you to open your eyes and look at me,
This is yours, all of me,
So, I rub my breast as you watch, leaning my head back,
I feel the bass drop,
You're correlating my ass like two cantaloupes,
I melt,
Into your hands, but I demand,
You put your hands to your side,
And again, close your eyes,
To your surprise, I'm not done,
Because it's not me whose getting pleased,
I take my hands from my breast and
put them on your chest,
I lean back down,
Rubbing my lips on yours,
You feel the wetness that's dripping from me,
I tell you to hold me as I put you inside,
My kitty,
She's purring,
I kiss your neck, as I glide you in and out,
Without a doubt,
You feel so good,
I wish I could make this momentum,
Taking my time to make this orgasm last,

I cam and I called out your name,
You looked at me and smelled but after while,
I'm not done,
I put one foot on the bed to make you cum,
I'm pounding that dick,
Put a wave in my body,
I put the other foot on the bed,
Got damn I feel so naughty,
Your penetrating this kitty,
About to give me your reward,
You tell me your about to explode,
So I jump off that dick to get what is owed,
I go ham on that meat,
This isn't for show,
He's King I'm Queen he's got to know,
I want all this cum to go,
Down my throat,
No drops a waist,
My baby,
Oh goodness,
I love the way he tastes,
But I'm not done I have one more to cum,
Playing with my vertical smile as you watch,
You lean over and kiss me,
And take over,
Inserting your finger,
Oh, baby it's about over,
You get up and put that dick in me,
Even though you had nothing left,
You wanted me to cum on that dick,
I looked at you with tears in my eyes,
Letting you know you're about to get your prize,

I put my feet on your cafes,
And I move my hips to sing with your song,
I grabbed you so tight,
I cam to your rhythm,
I loosened up my grip,
You looked and smiled,
Now turn your ass over so I can fuck you doggy style,
I did obey,
I put that ass up so you can play,
That dick went in,
You fuck me to no end,
Multiple orgasms I send,
You cam in my kitty,
You let out a grunt,
You clinched my hips,
My back dips down,
I feel you wipe the sweat from my crown,
You lay next to me, and I wipe your sweat from your head,
You said kiss me, baby,
That was the last thing you said.
Sleep.

YOUR TOWN

My words and my cognitive thinking grew
as I unlearned the lies that were told,
To us,
Only to control,
In us,
Those pagan ways that petrary who I'm not,
Who I will never be,
Controlled by your enslaved knowledge,
Drinking the wisdom that you once taught us,
About us,
Not seeing a black face among my towns
painting, statues, and names,
Engraved in the bricks, walls, or signs
that you polished and branded,
Made to fit your reality,
I see nothing that resembles me,
My melanin,
Is an absentee of this place that I call home,
Forcing your windows upon us,
To kill us off,
One by one
A tribe by a tribe,
slowly we rise,
Uniting beyond your reach
As we learn and teach,
Our young to understand,
What we read in those school books,
Are lies,

Nothing to retain,
Save your mental space,
To learn and trace,
The real history of our nationality,
No other can tell us or take.

ENERGY BEARING

You Bruthas look at my sistahs,
What is the first thought that comes to your mind?
What's between her thick thighs, what
that pussy feels like on your dick,
How does her body move?
Can you Bruthas think of anything but wanting to fuck?
Damn,
Elevate your cognitive thinking,
Physical is outward seeing,
Feel her soul in your hands,
Lay in bed with her mind,
Spiritually embracing her,
Don't be blind to the awakened woman,
She sees more than just fuckin,
Lusting your body is the last thing that she needs,
Fucking your pineal gland,
Strengthening her cells that drip from her vessel,
You're so camouflaged,
But we see right through You.

IN A WORD "LIFE"

Hurt,
The pain,
Sympathy,
Empathy,
The rain,
Rage,
The storm under my feet,
The reality of the norm,
Frustration,
The tides,
The questions,
The whys,
The smiles,
The fakes,
The rich,
I hate,
Love and anger,
Your eyes,
Your weather,
It is love or lust,
Your life and blind trust,
The pressure,
The games,
We mastered the insane,
The poor,
The homeless,
Ignorance of being kind,
The thoughtless,

The beautiful,
The pressures,
The stress,
Escaping the threats,
Societies eye,
Cheating,
Being investable,
Be it,
Life.

BEING

Minuscule particles that rotate my symbolic birth,
Underlying the myriad oscillating
force pyramid to my third eye,
Acceptance,
Of my natural form,
Emerging my 4 to my 1 and 9,
I'm a being of faith,
I'm spirituality embraced,
Grounded, yet not encased,
By your logic's or the materials that this world embrace,
The ratio of my circumference cannot be expressed,
Remotely don't channel me,
Logically,
I exercise my mentality to dance around your ignorance,
The oblivious astronomical force that preludes you,
Catalyzes your consciousness to only
take human imperfections,
Deludes you,
Oxidase your numerology,
Understand your biology,
Except the things you can't change,
Understand interchange,
Your range,
Of knowledge the being.

READ ME

Forward me the seeds of wisdom,
allow me to melt in the secret teachings, the Akashic
records holds the information that I need,
so, proceed, to the bounty of your manuscript.

NO MORE

Write my verse and touch my verbs to your
eyes, may it be attempted to breathe liquid
justified, dwell in inside my secluded wall,
lavished with webs unseen,
but a tone that's felt,
I can't be helped,
So, I stay till the noise goes silent.

SURVEY SAYS

Curly gold hair,
hazel brown eyes,
some call me thick,
social media call me obese,
however, I am beautiful through my eyes,
I don't bare all for all to see,
I don't shake my ass for the cameras
so you can downgrade me,
I am the girl next door,
the one you skip over,
to get to the best friend for,
I am my vision of me.

TALK TO ME

I fold, only to succumb to your gravitational pull, tasting the delicacy of the juices that secrets from you, I adorn you, venting my frustrations on to your body, charting the sweetness of the words your vessel projects, erect into me, aggressively, but passionately, I submit to thee.

REFLECTING

Venture into the forest of my soul,
You chopped down my virtue to the root,
Rain drops of leaves carpets my bark,
Why do you have to bury me from my world?

AS I SEE, I REMEMBER.

I'm at peace, however is peace realistic?

AUTHOR'S BIOGRAPHY

Sh'khinah Ma'at Sophia Yisreal is the author of these impressionable poems. She has a B.S. in biology at Martin University and her M.B.S at Indiana Wesleyan University. She has been involved with NOBECCE since 2017 and The Writing Center since 2020. She currently lives in Indiana. maatthepoet@gmail.com

Printed in the United States
By Bookmasters